My Favorite Tree

Terrific Trees of North America

Written & Illustrated
by Diane Iverson

J
582.16
I 94 m

Dawn Publications

HARTFORD DISCARD LIBRARY

Copyright © 1999 Diane Iverson
A Sharing Nature With Children Book

All rights reserved. No part of this book may be reproduced or transmitted to any form
or by any means, electronic or mechanical, including photocopying, recording, or by
any information and retrieval system, without written permission from the publisher.

Library of Congress Cataloging-in-Publication Data

Iverson, Diane.
My favorite tree : terrific trees of North America / written and illustrated by Diane
Iverson. — 1st ed.
p. cm.

Includes bibliographical references (p. 62) and index.
Summary: Examines the traits and uses of twenty-six North American trees, from the
ash to the yew, and describes notable or historic specimens.

ISBN 1-883220-94-7 (hardcover). — ISBN 1-883220-93-9 (pbk.)

1. Trees—United States—Juvenile literature. 2. Historic trees—United States—
Juvenile literature. 3. Trees—Canada—Juvenile literature. 4. Historic trees—
Canada—Juvenile literature. [1. Trees. 2. Historic trees.] I. Title. II. Series.
QK475.8.I94   1999
582.16'0973—dc21

98-47623
CIP
AC

Dawn Publications
14618 Tyler Foote Road
Nevada City, CA 95959
800-545-7475
Email: DawnPub@oro.net
Website: www.DawnPub.com

Printed in Hong Kong on recycled paper
10 9 8 7 6 5 4 3 2 1

First Edition

Computer production by Rob Froelick
Illustrations are in Prismacolor and Verithin pencils

My Favorite Tree

Terrific Trees of North America

In memory of my grandfather, James Virgil Wall, and
in honor of my grandmother, Lula Mae Wall,
the sturdy roots of my family tree.

He is like a tree planted beside a watercourse,
which yields its fruit in season and its leaf never withers:
in all that he does he prospers. Psalm 1:3

Acknowledgments

I want to thank the many people who helped during the creation of this book. My husband, Doug Iverson, worked as hard as I did and then cooked dinner. Kristin McDaniel, Rev. Eric Scott, Yaeko Tengan, Shirley Angel and Wayne Grossman assisted with research. Thanks especially to K. Nicholson and her students at Burcham School.

Across the areas covered by this book, park naturalists and other experts have shared in ways that enriched this project and my pleasure in doing it.

I also thank the following: Amy and Lindsay Aymar, Vanessa Bottorf, Cassandra and Lee Brown, David Brown, Holly Buliziuk, Virginia Burton, Todd Calhoun, Bill Cannon, Michael Coffin, Johnny and Lindsay Cook, Don Danielson, Amanda and Ashley Darnell, Carole Dermody, Jeff, Katy and Leigh Downing, Bob and Joyce Fisk, Carrie, Katie and Kirt Gartner, Chuck and Charlyn Glenn, Pat Graham, Glenna Hoff, Lorna Lang, Michele McDaniel, Tom Paquette, Clayton and Micky Parker, Jacy and Haleigh Petropoulos, Robert C. Power, Jr., Richard Ramon, Amy Reuter, Aaron and Tyler Riley, Lacey Rogers, Riley Scott, Helen and Billie Spell, David S. Teague, Mara Trushell, Lee-Anne Walker and Tom Wilder. Blessings on each of you!

There will always be the possibility of mistakes. I manage those without help from anyone. If you find one, I hope to hear from you.

Contents

All trees in this book are native to Canada, Mexico or the United States (including Hawaii). Trees introduced from other areas of the world are not covered. The variety of trees in North America is so terrific that not all could be chosen. Representative trees and tree families have been chosen for their natural beauty, for the varied geographic areas and habitats they represent, for their contribution to the balance of nature and for their many important human and wildlife uses. Champion trees have been chosen by combining measurements for height, circumference and spread.

My favorite tree
is the Green Ash. I love to
sit in its cool shade while I
write my special thoughts
and memories.

Ash

Green Ash — Olive Family

Tree Traits

Habitat: The Green Ash (*Fraxinus pennsylvanica*) is the most wide-spread native Ash in North America, covering most of eastern and central U.S. and Canada. It grows below 3000 feet on floodplains and along streams.

Height: The Green Ash generally grows to 60 feet.

Bark: Green Ash bark is dark gray, rough, scaly, and deeply furrowed, exposing a rusty-colored inner bark.

Leaves: Bright young leaves appear first in the spring. Each leaf consists of 7 to 9 leaflets that are 2 to 4 inches each. They are almost stemless. The elongated oval leaflets are toothed from middle to pointed tip, shiny green on top and lighter below. They turn bright yellow before dropping.

Flowers & Seeds: Young leaves are followed by clusters of tiny green flowers. Male and female flowers grow on different trees. Clustered, winged seeds called "keys" mature in autumn and drift away on the wind. The seed with its thin, dry, papery wing looks a bit like a small key.

Wild Companions

Although it is not a major food source for North American wildlife, the Green Ash contributes to the diet of several species. Pine grosbeaks, wild turkeys, bobwhite quail, purple finches, and **red crossbills** are among the birds that feed on ash keys (winged seeds). The industrious, sturdy-toothed beaver chomps away at the bark, and both

mule and white-tailed deer browse its twigs and foliage. Seeds of a water-loving relative, the Swamp-privet, are eaten by ducks. Branches and foliage also provide a good nesting site for many birds.

It's a Fact

❖ Sioux Indians used ash to carve prayer pipes. The pipe, called a *Chanupa,* also had a bowl of soapstone. The stone represented the spirits of their departed ancestors, and the ash represented the spirits of nature. When using the pipe they asked for the wisdom of both their ancestors and the spirits of nature to help them make decisions.

❖ Native Americans in northern regions used ash to make snow shoes, bending it into shape by heating it over a fire while still green.

❖ European settlers used the inner bark of Blue Ash to make a blue dye and the strong ash wood for farm tools like harrows and rakes.

❖ White Ash, a strong, shock-resistant wood, is used to make sports equipment like baseball bats, oars and hockey sticks.

Hall of Fame

The U.S. national champion Green Ash is in Cass City, Michigan. Its trunk measures over 21 feet in circumference, its height is 95 feet, and it has a spread of 95 feet.

Some Olive Family Members

White Ash

Velvet Ash

Green Ash

Mexican Ash

I like to hear Aspen leaves rustle
and sing in the wind. Listening
to their music makes me
feel so peaceful.

Aspen
Quaking Aspen — Willow Family

Tree Traits

Habitat: The Quaking Aspen (*Populus tremuloides*) has the widest geographic range of any North American tree. It is native to much of Canada, Alaska, and the northeastern U.S. It is also found scattered throughout the western U.S. and northern Mexico up to 10,000 feet elevation, often in pure groves. It is also widely planted as an ornamental.

Height: The Aspen generally grows to 100 feet.

Bark: The whitish-green or cream-colored bark is thin, with warty horizontal markings. Older trees may have heavily furrowed gray bark on lower trunks.

Leaves: Aspen leaves are almost round with toothed edges and short points, 1 to 4 inches long. They are bright green above, lighter below. Leaves turn golden or sometimes bright reddish-orange before dropping in the fall. The stem is long and flat.

Flowers & seeds: Male and female catkins appear on different trees in early spring before trees leaf out. Drooping clusters of catkins, as long as 4 inches, hold many $1/2$ inch capsules filled with tiny, fibrous seeds. These seeds mature in late spring. Trees most often reproduce from young shoots that come up from roots of established trees.

Wild Companions

Ruffed grouse feed on young buds and leaves while **broad-tailed hummingbirds** perch on their tiny lichen-covered nests. Hungry black bears, mule and white-tailed deer, elk, bighorn sheep and moose browse tender shoots and foliage. Aspen is important to the beaver, who eats its twigs and bark and uses it as construction material for its lodge. The tender bark of snow-bent twigs and branches provides winter food for the snowshoe hare. Yellow-bellied sapsuckers drill rows of small holes, called wells, on trunks. They drink the sap along with insects that are attracted to it.

It's a Fact

❖ Native Americans of the plains, plateau and northern forests used straight trees like Aspen and Lodgepole Pine for tepee poles. When nomadic groups traveled, these same trees became travois poles, stretched out behind horses to carry belongings.

❖ Native Americans chewed the inner bark of the aspen and other willow trees to relieve aches and pains. Settlers made tea from it for the same reason. Aspen was considered soothing to the throat and stomach. It was made into a cough syrup or laxative. Scientists later discovered that the bark contains salicylic acid, the active ingredient in aspirin.

❖ An entire aspen grove is likely to rise from one single root system, making each new tree an exact clone of an individual ancient ancestor. Because of this connection, whole groves take on their fall color at the same time.

❖ Aspen is planted as an ornamental because of its attractive white bark and striking golden foliage.

Hall of Fame

The U.S. national champion Quaking Aspen is in Ontonagon, Michigan, measuring 10 feet in circumference, 109 feet tall, with a spread of 59 feet.

Some Willow Family Members

Quaking Aspen

Black Willow

White Willow

Beak Willow

Bigtooth Aspen

My favorite tree is
the Paper Birch. I like to
write letters on pieces of its
curly, white bark. It makes
every letter special.

Birch
Paper Birch — Birch Family

Tree Traits

Habitat: Paper Birch *(Betula papyrifera)* grows where there is moist soil and available sunlight, often in pure groves with an interconnected root system, throughout the northern U.S., Canada, and in Alaska.

Height: Birches commonly grow to 80 feet.

Bark: The Paper Birch is named for its thin, white bark with horizontal markings, curling off in papery strips to show pale rusty or tan inner bark; may be dark and furrowed at the base. Cutting the bark causes an unsightly black scar; it peels naturally in strips that can be found on the ground.

Leaves: Birch leaves are oval with a rounded base and pointed tip, $1\frac{1}{2}$ to 5 inches long, dark green on top, pale yellow-green below, with coarse, uneven teeth. They turn yellow before falling in autumn.

Flowers & seeds: Male and female flowers called catkins grow on the same tree in late spring before the appearance of young leaves. Hanging cones, holding tiny seeds with silky plumes, mature in autumn, then fall apart.

Wild Companions

The caterpillar of the huge **luna moth**

feeds primarily on birch leaves. Beaver eat bark and twigs, and snowshoe hares also nibble at the bark of Paper Birch. Its twigs are part of the winter diet of the moose. Yellow-bellied sapsuckers tap little holes in the bark for sap wells, using their special brush-like tongues to gather the liquid. Redpolls are among the many birds that eat the catkins in spring. Seeds are eaten by titmice, juncos, finches, and other birds.

It's a Fact

❖ The famous birch-bark canoe was a light, graceful canoe made by Native Americans of the Great Lakes region. Canoe frames were made of Northern White Cedar, covered with large sheets of Birch bark which might be sewn with Black Spruce root and

sealed with pitch from pine or spruce. The pinkish inner bark always faced the outside of the canoe.

❖ Ojibwa, Algonquin, Huron and Micmac tribes made containers from the bark, which they sometimes decorated with dyed moose hair or porcupine quill embroidery.

❖ Some tribes recorded their creation stories, prayers, songs and sacred teachings on birch-bark scrolls.

Hall of Fame

Paper Birch is the state tree of New Hampshire. The U.S. national championship for Paper Birch is shared by two trees. One, in Cheboygan City, Michigan, is 18 feet in circumference, 107 feet tall and has a spread of 76 feet. The other is in Point Aux Barques, Michigan. It is 18 feet in circumference, 107 feet tall and has a 76 foot spread.

Some Birch Family Members

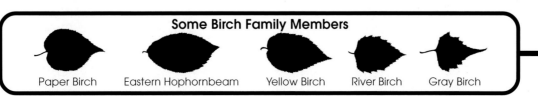

Paper Birch   Eastern Hophornbeam   Yellow Birch   River Birch   Gray Birch

11

My Red Cedar brings visitors right to my window.

Cedar
Eastern Red Cedar — Cypress Family

Tree Traits

Habitat: The Eastern Red Cedar (*Juniperus virginiana*) is a well adapted tree, more widely distributed than any other conifer in the eastern U.S. It is native to a variety of sites, from dry hillsides to open fields or swampland, throughout most of the eastern U.S., as far west as Texas, and in southern-most Canada. It is also planted as an ornamental.

Height: The Eastern Red Cedar generally grows to 60 feet.

Bark: The Cedar has light reddish-brown, thin bark, with stringy fibers that separate into long flaky strips.

Leaves: Rows of tiny, scale-like, evergreen leaves give the appearance of braided green twigs on older growth. On young branches leaves may be as much as $1/4$ inch long and spread more like needles.

Flowers & Seeds: In spring the male trees release pollen from their small papery cones, giving them a yellow-brown hue. The fleshy cones of the female trees look like frosty blue berries. Although they are little more than $1/4$ inch in diameter, they give the tree a blue tone in fall and winter.

Wild Companions

The masked **cedar waxwing** was so named because of its fondness for

the juicy blue cones of the female tree. Many other song birds and game birds, including the purple finch, mockingbird, robin, bluebird, wild turkey, bobwhite, quail and eastern kingbird enjoy the fruit as well. Many birds nest or roost in the foliage.

It's a Fact

❖ Because cedar wood is resistant to decay, early colonists used it for log cabins and fences. It was used to make butter churns and milk buckets as well. The wood is also used to make moth-proof cedar chests.

❖ Some people consider the smoke of slowly burning cedar leaves to be spiritually cleansing. The Seminole people of the southeast valued incense made from cedar leaves to cleanse evil from their dwellings.

❖ Other members of the Cypress family, like the Western Red Cedar, had many Native American uses. Natives of the northern Pacific Coast region used cedar to carve and paint totem poles and masks like this Raven ceremonial mask. Its wood is soft, perfect for hollowing out dugout canoes. Shredded bark was twisted into string and made into clothing and sleeping mats.

Hall of Fame

The U.S. champion Eastern Red Cedar is 20 feet in circumference, 57 feet tall and has a spread of 69 feet. It is in Coffee City, Georgia.

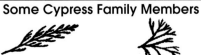

Some Cypress Family Members

| Eastern Red Cedar | Incense Cedar | Atlantic White Cedar | Alligator Juniper |

The Cherry is my favorite tree—one for me and one for the pie, one for me and one for the pie!

Cherry
Black Cherry — Rose Family

Tree Traits

Habitat: Black Cherry *(Prunus serotina)* grows throughout the eastern U.S., into eastern Canada, scattered through portions of the southwestern states and in portions of Mexico. It grows in mixed hardwood forests where there is open sunlight. It can be found as high as 7,500 feet elevation.

Height: The Black Cherry generally grows to 100 feet.

Bark: On young trees the bark is smooth and reddish-purple. It will become rough, with dark gray curled chips, as trees age.

Leaves: Black Cherry leaves are narrow, finely-toothed and pointed, 2 to 6 inches long, shiny, dark green above and lighter below. Come autumn, leaves turn gold or red before falling.

Flowers & Seeds: In late spring, white flowers are scattered down delicate, drooping stems in graceful clusters. Each individual blossom is less than $1/2$ inch wide and has five petals. Petals soon scatter like snow. They will be replaced by small cherries that turn from red to black as they ripen in late summer.

Wild Companions

The Black Cherry provides a feast for wildlife. The caterpillar of the tiger swallowtail devours its leaves. The rose-breasted grosbeak nips off the tender bases of cherry blossoms. Other birds like the robin, eastern bluebird, cedar waxwing , wood thrush and sharp-tailed grouse love cherries. Raccoons, opossums and foxes join in. Chipmunks and white-footed mice scurry for their share, too.

Black bears climb the trees to get them, often breaking branches. The leaves are poisonous to cattle if eaten in large amounts.

It's a Fact

❖ The Black Cherry is our largest native cherry tree. Since pioneer times, people have used wild cherries to make juice, jelly, wine, breads and cherry pie. They are a bit tart, but they can be eaten fresh as well.

❖ A bark extract was used by Native Americans for coughs and sore throats. Black Cherry cough syrup is still made from the bark.

❖ Native Americans of the Pacific Northwest cut strips of the rusty-brown colored bark of the Common Chokecherry (a relative) to weave into their baskets as decorations.

❖ This strong, beautiful, reddish-brown wood is prized for fine furniture, paneling and cabinetry. It is second only to Black Walnut in popularity.

❖ Young George Washington once admitted cutting down a cherry tree with his hatchet.

Hall of Fame

The U.S. national champion Black Cherry is 17 feet in circumference, 134 feet tall and has a spread of 70 feet. It can be found in Great Smoky Mountains National Park, in Tennessee.

Some Rose Family Members

| Black Cherry | Holly Leaf Cherry | Toyon | Carolina Laurelcherry |

HARTFORD PUBLIC LIBRARY

I love to float
Cottonwood leaves,
like little yellow boats,
on the shallows at
the river's edge.

Cottonwood
Fremont Cottonwood — Willow Family

Tree Traits

Habitat: Fremont Cottonwood (*Populus fremontii*) grows along watered areas in the arid southwestern U.S. and northern Mexico.

Height: The Fremont Cottonwood grows to 80 feet.

Bark: The thick, light gray bark is rough-textured with irregular furrows. Smaller branches have smooth white-green bark.

Leaves: Light green and shiny, these triangular leaves are roughly-toothed and have long flat stems. They are 2 to 3 inches in diameter. They turn golden yellow in autumn.

Flowers & Seeds: Long, slender flowers called catkins appear on the cottonwood in early spring. Male and female catkins grow on different trees. Glossy yellow-green leaves appear next. Small oval fruit ripens along the female catkin later in spring, each opening into three sections. Seeds from these tiny capsules are carried on the wind by the cottony fibers, or down, that give this tree its name. Leaves turn bright yellow in fall, dropping off until the winter cottonwood is a stark gray skeleton.

Wild Companions

The caterpillar of the **mourning cloak butterfly** feeds on cottonwood

leaves. The colorful vermilion flycatcher often uses the fork of a cottonwood branch as a base for its nest of grass and spider webs, feeding on neighborhood insects. The summer tanager and Rivoli's hummingbird also nest here. Calliope hummingbirds use soft cottonwood down to line their tiny nests. Mule deer browse the foliage and porcupine eat twigs and tender inner bark. Beaver use it as dam building material. They also eat the bark.

It's a Fact

❖ The Hopi and Zuni of the southwest carve intricate Kachina dolls from the soft roots of the Fremont Cottonwood. These dolls represent a spirit being. They bring more deer or antelope, make boys into good hunters or warn young children to behave. The Black Ogre Kachina is said to kidnap naughty children. The Bee Kachina gives cups of honey to young children at certain dance ceremonies, but he also dances around shooting people with a miniature bow and blunt arrow, just as a real bee might sting them. Monster Woman catches children with a long hooked staff and threatens to chop off their heads with her knife.

❖ Pick a small cottonwood twig and let it dry for a couple of weeks. Snap it open at a joint or growth line, and you will find a perfect five-pointed star inside!

Hall of Fame

Two willow family members are state trees. The Balsam Poplar is the state tree of Wyoming, and the Eastern Cottonwood represents Kansas. The U.S. national champion Fremont Cottonwood is 42 feet in circumference, 92 feet tall and has a 108 foot spread. It is located in Santa Cruz City, Arizona.

Some Willow Family Members

Eastern Cottonwood | Fremont Cottonwood | Quaking Aspen | Balsam Poplar | Narrowleaf Cottonwood

I gathered a bouquet
from our backyard
Dogwood tree for
our neighbor. I do
it every year.

Dogwood
Flowering Dogwood — Dogwood Family

Tree Traits

Habitat: Flowering Dogwood (*Cornus florida*) is found through much of the eastern U.S. at elevations up to 5000 feet. Dogwoods grow underneath larger trees in deciduous forests but can also be found in clearings.

Height: The Dogwood generally grows to 35 feet.

Bark: Its bark is reddish brown and broken into small scaly blocks on mature trees.

Leaves: Oval, pointed leaves have edges that are somewhat wavy, $2^{1}/_{2}$ to 5 inches long. Stems are short and veins are curved toward the leaf tip. Leaves turn bright scarlet to deep purple, or sometimes yellow, before falling.

Flowers & Seeds: Small button-shaped buds for spring flowers can be found on the bare tree even in winter. Miniature flower clusters, surrounded by four large white bracts are commonly called flowers. They create a graceful and showy display in early spring before leaves develop. Leaves are followed by bright clusters of shiny scarlet fruit in autumn, each about $^{1}/_{2}$ inch in diameter.

Wild Companions

Dogwood is a common host plant for hungry caterpillars of the beautiful **spring azure butterfly**. The summer

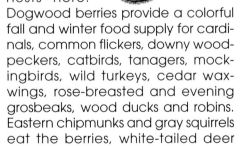

tanager nests here. Dogwood berries provide a colorful fall and winter food supply for cardinals, common flickers, downy woodpeckers, catbirds, tanagers, mockingbirds, wild turkeys, cedar waxwings, rose-breasted and evening grosbeaks, wood ducks and robins. Eastern chipmunks and gray squirrels eat the berries, white-tailed deer munch on the leaves, and the eastern cottontail nibbles at the inner bark for winter nourishment.

It's a Fact

❖ Because they were straight, dogwood shoots were often used by Native Americans of the northern woodlands for arrows. They were peeled, smoothed, then split at the tip where arrowheads of stone, horn, bone or iron were attached with sinew. Split and trimmed feathers were attached along the shaft to help the arrow fly straight.

❖ Native Americans extracted red dye from dogwood roots to create designs in basket materials. The Yuki and Yana peoples of central California combined the shoots and twigs of the Pacific Dogwood, Willow and Redbud to weave decorative cradles.

❖ Colonists brewed a medicinal tea from the bark as a treatment for fever.

Hall of Fame

Flowering Dogwood is the state tree of Missouri and Virginia and the state flower of Virginia and North Carolina. The U.S. national championship for Flowering Dogwoods is shared by two trees. The first, in Norfolk, Virginia, is 9 feet in circumference, 33 feet tall and has a spread of 42 feet. The second, in Sampson City, North Carolina, is $9^{1}/_{2}$ feet in circumference, 31 feet tall and has a 48 foot spread.

Some Dogwood Family Members

Flowering Dogwood   Roughleaf Dogwood   Red Osier Dogwood   Pacific Dogwood

My favorite tree is the
beautiful Elm. Many Elms
died from a terrible disease, but
they are making a comeback.
I'm making a comeback, too.

Elm
American Elm — Elm Family

Tree Traits

Habitat: American Elm *(Ulmus americana)* is native to mixed deciduous forests in the eastern half of the U.S. and Canada. It prefers rich, moist soils at lower elevations. With its gracefully spreading crown, it has been planted well beyond its natural range. Once plentiful, many have been wiped out by disease.

Height: The Elm often grows to 90 feet.

Bark: Elm bark is thick, light gray, and deeply furrowed with random forks and heavily textured ridges.

Leaves: Uneven at their base, leaves are oval and toothed with pointed tips, 3 to 6 inches long. Young leaves are pale green, turning dark green as they mature, then turn bright, golden yellow in the fall.

Flowers & Seeds: Clusters of tiny, cup-shaped flowers appear before leaves show, giving the tree a lavender halo. Fruit, called keys, hangs in clusters. Each long stem holds one small seed inside a flat, oval, papery wing with hair along its edges.

Wild Companions

Elm trees buzz with the music of honey bees when they bloom in early spring. Caterpillars of several butterflies—the comma tortoise shell, the painted lady and the red admiral—are among several species that feed on elm leaves. Birds such as the purple finch, black-capped chickadee and wild turkey, eat the papery seeds and tender buds, as do mammals like the eastern fox-squirrel. Another bird, the yellow-bellied sapsucker, makes little holes in the bark so it can drink the sap. The colorful **Baltimore oriole** nests in its branches.

It's a Fact

❖ Many of these shapely trees have been killed by Dutch Elm disease, introduced accidentally to the U.S. in a French shipment of contaminated elm logs in 1931. This devastating fungus is carried by European and American Elm bark beetles. Agricultural researchers are developing disease-resistant clones of the American Elm and there is hope for this great tree.

❖ Iroquois Indians constructed elm bark canoes by attaching the sturdy, flexible sheets of bark to strong wooden frames. Seams were stitched tightly with small, split roots and sealed with pitch. Elm bark canoes were not as fast as birch-bark canoes, but they were strong. Iroquois longhouses were built with elm poles covered with sheets of elm bark.

❖ Because the wood bends well, it is used for barrels and for furniture, such as bentwood chairs.

❖ As a young man in the mid-1700s, George Washington planted an American Elm in Berkeley Springs, West Virginia. That elm still stands today.

Hall of Fame

The American Elm is the state tree of Massachusetts and North Dakota. The U.S. national champion is in Grand Traverse City, Michigan, and is 23 feet in circumference, 112 feet tall, with a spread of 115 feet.

Some Elm Family Members

American Elm | Canyon Hackberry | Winged Elm | Cedar Elm | Water Elm

My favorite tree is the Holly. I pick its shiny leaves and red berries to make a cheery wreath for our front door.

Holly
American Holly — Holly Family

Tree Traits

Habitat: The Holly *(Ilex opaca)* grows at low elevations in mixed deciduous forests, especially on floodplains. Native to the southeastern U.S., it is a popular ornamental addition to many yards elsewhere.

Height: Mature Holly trees vary from 40 to 70 feet.

Bark: Holly bark is light gray and thin. It may be smooth or bumpy.

Leaves: These leaves are distinctive—thick and tough, shiny dark green on their top surface and lighter underneath, 2 to 4 inches long. They are evergreen, with sharp, prickly edges.

Flowers & Seeds: Small, white flower clusters appear in spring. Male and female flowers, each with four petals, look similar but are on separate trees. Green, berry-like fruit, barely over ¼ inch in diameter, appears on female trees. These smooth-skinned, fleshy berries, each containing four small brown seeds, will turn shiny red in the fall, and remain attached during the winter.

Wild Companions

Honey bees visit this tree when it is in bloom, foraging for nectar. Caterpillars of the spring azure butterfly feed on the leaves.

Many small birds feed on the bitter berries of the female tree, especially hermit thrushes, robins, wood thrushes, cedar waxwings and northern mockingbirds. Flocks of wild turkeys take advantage of these berries, too. Among mammals, opossums, white-tailed deer and raccoons feed on holly fruit. The thick, prickly, evergreen foliage provides excellent shelter for nesting and roosting of small birds.

It's a Fact

❖ Many people collect holly branches in December because the leaves and berries are popular for wreaths and other holiday floral decorations. Some varieties are cultivated in orchards for this purpose.

❖ Although the bitter fruit is not eaten by humans, the colorful berries make trees of the holly family a welcome addition to yards and gardens. They are also popular because they attract so much wildlife.

❖ Cabinetmakers and carvers prize the fine-grained, ivory-colored wood.

❖ Ancient Romans believed holly protected them from evil spirits. In early England holly was believed to protect households from witches, rabid dogs and other evils.

Hall of Fame

The American Holly is the state tree of Delaware. The title for U.S. national champion is shared by three trees. The Holly in Chambers City, Alabama, is almost ten feet in circumference, 74 feet high and has a 48 foot spread. One from Buckingham City, Virginia, is 11 feet in circumference, 55 feet high and has a 51 foot spread. The third, in Brunswick, Georgia, is over 8 feet in circumference, 89 feet tall and has a spread of 63 feet.

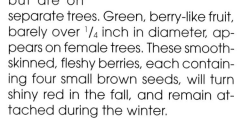

Some Holly Family Members

American Holly Dahoon Myrtle Dahoon Yaupon Mountain Winterberry

The Honeylocust is a
giving tree—it gives lots
of sweet seed pods in
the fall for hungry
animals to eat.

Honeylocust
Honeylocust — Legume Family

Tree Traits

Habitat: The Honeylocust (*Gleditsia triacanthos*) lives between the Great Lakes and eastern Texas. It prefers moist bottomlands but survives in a variety of settings.

Height: The Honeylocust grows to 80 feet.

Bark: This bark is dull brown to gray with long, narrow flat plates, and here and there are large clusters of stiff, forked spines or thorns with multiple points.

Leaves: Honeylocust leaves are delicate and lacy, shiny dark green on top, yellow-green below. They grow in 5 to 8 inch long compound or doubly compound clusters, with as many as thirty $1/2$ to $1^1/2$ inch leaflets in a cluster. Autumn leaves turn yellow before dropping.

Flowers & Seeds: Small, very fragrant, yellow-green flowers appear in short clusters, sprouting from leaf bases in early spring. Male and female clusters are often on separate twigs or trees. Large, deep brown, twisted pods as long as 18 inches contain dark oval seeds. They mature in the fall and drop in late autumn.

Wild Companions

Honey bees take nectar from this family of trees in the spring. The silver-spotted skipper butterfly lays its eggs on the upper side of honeylocust leaves. When the eggs hatch as caterpillars, they are sitting on their dinner! The large, sweet pods provide fall and winter food to a variety of wildlife including **rabbits**, deer, foxes, squirrels and birds. Cattle also graze on them. They are an important survival food during winter, when finding something to eat can be difficult.

It's a Fact

❖ This tree gets its name from the honey-like sweetness of the pulp inside the young pod which was chewed as a treat by pioneer children.

❖ Some family members are beautiful ornamentals, such as the New Mexico Locust, with its drooping clusters of fragrant purplish-pink blossoms.

❖ The strong, hard, decay-resistant wood is used for railroad ties and construction. Because it is not abundant, it is not widely marketed.

❖ During his lifetime, Barry Mayes, of Prescott, Arizona, grew from seeds and gave away roughly 1,000 Honeylocust trees, making a lasting environmental contribution to the town, and showing what one dedicated person can do.

Hall of Fame

The U.S. national championship for Honeylocust is shared by three trees. The first, located in Lenawee, Michigan, is $16^1/2$ feet in circumference, 116 feet tall and has a spread of 104 feet. The Greencastle, Pennsylvania, champion is 19 feet in circumference, 90 feet tall and has an 88 foot spread. The third, from Botetourt City, Virginia, is 18 feet in circumference, 104 feet tall and has an 84 foot spread.

Some Legume Family Members

Honeylocust

New Mexico Locust

Black Locust

My favorite tree is the
Joshua Tree because it
is so weird and different
from any other tree.

Joshua Tree
Joshua Tree — Lily Family

Tree Traits

Habitat: The odd Joshua Tree *(Yucca brevifolia)* is the unique, identifying plant of the Mojave Desert. It grows in dry soils of a small region of the southwest to 6,000 feet. It is also planted as an interesting ornamental in other desert regions.

Height: The Joshua Tree generally grows to 30 feet.

Bark: Its bark is gray and roughly broken into plates.

Leaves: Joshua Tree leaves are 8 to14 inch long stiff spears or daggers with sharp points and finely-toothed edges growing in clusters. This is an evergreen tree.

Flowers & Seeds: Pale green, oval flowers as large as $1^1/_2$ inches appear from February to April. They grow in branched clusters, reaching $1^1/_2$ feet in height. Large, green fruit pods may reach 4 inches. They eventually turn brown, and have rows of neatly stacked flat black seeds. They ripen by late spring, falling to the ground unopened.

Wild Companions

The yucca moth is especially important to the Joshua Tree. It lays its eggs inside the flower, pollinating the tree. Birds, mule deer, and ground squirrels eat tender Joshua Tree blossoms. Red-tailed hawks and ravens perch high on branches to scout the area for a meal. Several birds use the trees as nesting sites. One bird, the **loggerhead shrike**, is not strong enough to tear apart the lizards that it catches—so, the bird pierces it on a spear-like leaf, and in a few days returns to fetch his dinner when it is more tender.

It's a Fact

❖ Sharp tips of Joshua Tree leaves were used by southwestern Native Americans to paint pottery designs.

❖ Hopi, Zuni, Apache and Yavapai Indians use the reddish inner bark strips, and reddish-brown inner fibers of the root in intricate basket designs.

❖ Decorated and hollowed stalks of the tree were made into single-string fiddles by the Apache.

❖ The Diegueno people twined the fibers together to make small cleaning brushes.

❖ The ancient Anasazi people used yucca fiber for woven sandals.

❖ Natives pounded the roots to create a sudsy soap.

❖ Cahuilla, Surrano and Chemehuevi people ate seeds of the Joshua Tree raw or ground them into flour.

Hall of Fame

The two champion trees are both in San Bernardino, California. One of them is 9 feet in circumference, 36 feet tall and has a 36 foot spread. The blossom of a relative, the Soaptree Yucca, is the state flower of New Mexico.

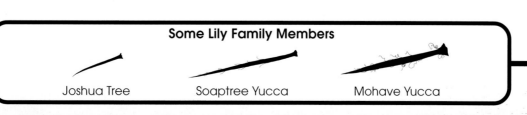

Some Lily Family Members

| Joshua Tree | Soaptree Yucca | Mohave Yucca |

My favorite smell is of
sweet Magnolia blossoms in
spring. I smell it all night long when
Mom and Dad let me camp
out underneath our tree.

Magnolia
Southern Magnolia — Magnolia Family

Tree Traits

Habitat: Southern Magnolia (*Magnolia grandiflora*) is native to the southeastern coastal states, ranging from North Carolina to eastern Texas, but is planted in moderate climates beyond its range. It prefers full sun and thrives in moist, fertile soils.

Height: The Southern Magnolia generally grows to 100 feet.

Bark: The Magnolia's bark is gray-brown and scaly.

Leaves: These leaves are tough and leathery, 5 to 8 inches long. They are a glossy, dark green on top, with a velvety rust tone on the underside. This is a broad-leaved evergreen tree.

Flowers & Seeds: Magnolia trees do not start to bloom until they are 10 to 20 years old. Fragrant white flowers as large as 8 inches in diameter open at the end of twigs by late spring or early summer. Fruit is light pinkish-brown and cone shaped, covered with small, shiny, bright red pods, each containing 2 to 3 seeds. These seed pods dangle from the fruit surface in autumn.

Wild Companions

The Southern Magnolia is not considered a vital food source for North American wildlife, but it supplies part of the diet of a number of species. Magnolia fruit is eaten by squirrels, **white-footed mice**, wild turkeys and various small birds. White-tailed deer forage twigs and leaves, and the yellow-bellied sapsucker busily drills wells in the bark for the sap. The Sweet Bay, a family member, is a host plant to caterpillars of the tiger swallowtail and spicebush swallowtail butterflies.

It's a Fact

❖ The magnolia's durable dried leaves are used in large flower arrangements.

❖ The Southern Magnolia, with its spectacular blossoms and large shiny leaves, was one of the American trees most prized in early European gardens. It also graced the gardens and grounds of America's old southern plantations. It remains popular in parks, gardens and street plantings.

❖ Andrew Jackson, the seventh U.S. President, planted a graceful Southern Magnolia near the South Portico of the White House in honor of his wife, Rachel.

❖ While many members of this family are evergreen, others, like the Cucumber Magnolia, Fraser Magnolia and Yellow Poplar, are deciduous, loosing their leaves in the fall.

Hall of Fame

Mississippi claims the showy Southern Magnolia as its state tree as well as its state flower. It is also the state flower of Louisiana. The Tulip Tree, a relative, is the state tree of Tennessee and Indiana. The U.S. national champion Southern Magnolia is over 22 feet in circumference, 98 feet tall, and it has a 90 foot spread. It grows in Jones City, Mississippi.

Some Magnolia Family Members

Southern Magnolia   Yellow Poplar   Cucumber Tree   Sweet Bay Magnolia   Umbrella Tree

My brother and I run and
jump into a pile of crunchy
Maple leaves. Then
Mom gives us hot
maple cookies.

Maple
Sugar Maple — Maple Family

Tree Traits

Habitat: Sugar Maple *(Acer saccharum)* is native throughout the northeastern quarter of the U.S. and into southeastern Canada.

Height: Maples generally grow to 100 feet.

Bark: Pale gray and thick, the bark has deep vertical furrows with rough, scaled ridges.

Leaves: These distinctive leaves have three to five lobes, with occasional large teeth at the edges, 3 to 6 inches in diameter. They are dark green above, lighter below. In fall, as weather cools, leaves turn brilliant shades of yellow, orange and red, coloring the eastern countryside until they fall.

Flowers & Seeds: Small yellow flowers hang from long, delicate stems in spring, and young maple leaves spread their lobes like tiny fingers. Soon winged seed cases form in pairs. When they ripen, they will gently twirl to the ground like miniature propellers as they drop from trees. Each seed case holds one seed.

Wild Companions

Maple flowers draw honey bees in the spring. Maple seeds and buds are also a valuable food source for many birds, including the evening grosbeak, purple finch, cardinal, sharp-tailed grouse, red crossbill and bobwhite quail. Small mammals such as the eastern chipmunk, eastern red squirrel and eastern gray squirrel get their share, too. The maple is also a host plant for caterpillars of the tiger swallowtail butterfly. White-tailed deer and moose browse tender branches and foliage. The **porcupine** nibbles at inner bark.

It's a Fact

❖ Algonquin, Iroquois and other native peoples of the Eastern woodlands harvested sap from Sugar Maples in early spring. It was then heated in hollowed-out logs by adding red-hot stones until it thickened into syrup. Colonists learned this skill from Native Americans. Thirty to forty gallons of sap is required to make one gallon of maple syrup. This natural bounty is still being harvested and enjoyed today.

❖ The beautifully grained wood of the maple tree is strong and shock-resistant. From Colonial times it has been prized for quality furniture. It is still one of America's most cherished hardwoods, used often for floors, cabinets, cutting blocks and furniture.

Hall of Fame

The Sugar Maple is the official national tree of Canada. Its leaf is the focal point of the Canadian flag, and is also used to decorate Canadian coins and stamps. The Sugar Maple is also the state tree of New York, Vermont, West Virginia and Wisconsin. The Red Maple is the state tree of Rhode Island. The U.S. national champion Sugar Maple is located in Kitzmiller, Maryland, and is $22^1/_2$ feet in circumference, 65 feet tall, and has a spread of 54 feet.

Some Maple Family Members

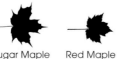   

| Sugar Maple | Red Maple | Rocky Mtn. Sugar Maple | Striped Maple | Silver Maple | Big Leaf Maple |

My special place is a crook
in a Bur Oak, where I go to
share my dreams and wishes.
My tree is good at
keeping secrets.

Oak
Bur Oak — Beech Family

Tree Traits

Habitat: The Bur Oak (*Quercus macrocarpa*) is found in central Canada and the U.S., south to Texas. It grows in dry, gravelly areas, but prefers well-drained floodplains, usually below 3000 feet.

Height: Bur Oaks generally grow to 100 feet.

Bark: Bur Oak bark is pale gray, thick, roughly-ridged and scaly.

Leaves: Narrow at the stem, the leaves have several rounded lobes on each side, with a broad tip. They are 4 to 12 inches long and shiny, dark green on top, with gray-green below. In autumn they turn yellow or brown.

Flowers & Seeds: Male and female flowers are found on the same tree in early spring. Acorns start out tiny and green but become the largest of over 55 species in North America. By fall, when they ripen to a soft brown, they are as long as $2^1/_4$ inches from stem to tip. Their deep, furry caps can cover more than half of the acorn.

The Bur Oak acorn dwarfs a normal sized acorn.

Wild Companions

Wild turkeys, blue jays, Steller's jays, **scrub jays**, wood ducks and red-bellied woodpeckers feast on acorn mast. The white-breasted nuthatch thrives on the tree's rich insect population as well as its acorns. Birds like the scarlet tanager often use an oak branch as a nesting site. The tiny tufted titmouse and much larger common grackle also rely on acorns for food. Black bears, raccoons, javalina (a pig-like animal) and gray squirrels are among the many mammals that depend on a variety of oaks for a portion of their diet.

It's a Fact

❖ Oak species are divided into two major groups: red oaks and white oaks. Because of their strength and hardness, white oaks are used for everything from barrels to furniture to ships and boats.

❖ Many native peoples gathered acorns in large collecting baskets and ground them into a meal that was made into small cakes. This was a dietary staple for California Natives.

❖ The Chestnut, a relative, was virtually eliminated in the early 1900s by Chestnut blight. Because this fungus kills only the portion of the tree growing above the ground, roots are still alive. New sprouts rise from these old stumps, but become diseased before they reach maturity. Botanists are trying to develop disease-resistant strains.

Hall Of Fame

Iowa chose all its native oaks as its state tree, including the Bur Oak. There is a town in Iowa named Bur Oak. New Jersey chose the Northern Red Oak; Washington, D.C. chose the Scarlet Oak. The U.S. national champion Bur Oak, in Paris, Kentucky, is almost 27 feet in circumference, 96 feet tall and has a spread of 103 feet.

Some Beech Family Members (see also Gambel Oak)

Bur Oak   American Beech   Black Oak   Valley Oak   Coast Live Oak   White Oak   Northern Red Oak

The Gambel Oak is where we have our secret tree fort.

No Boys Allowed!

Oak
Gambel Oak — Beech Family

Tree Traits

Habitat: The Gambel Oak (*Quercus gambelii*) is native to the southwestern U.S. and northern Mexico, found among Ponderosa Pine forests in mountain and plateau country at high elevations. In some parts of its range it can be shorter and more shrub-like, growing in dense thickets.

Height: Gambel Oaks generally grow to 70 feet.

Bark: Gambel Oak bark is thick, gray, roughly textured and furrowed.

Leaves: Two to 6 inches long, leaves are oblong and glossy dark green with several rounded lobes. Leaves turn yellow or dull reddish-brown and release from branches in autumn.

Fruits & Flowers: Tiny male and female flowers appear on the same tree in spring. New leaves develop at about the same time. Small green acorns form in the summer. The oval acorns of the Gambel Oak mature in one year, becoming ripe in the fall.

Wild Companions

The Gambel Oak is the host plant for the beautiful **Colorado Hairstreak butterfly**, while the javalina, wild turkeys and squirrels eat the acorns, and mule deer browse the foliage. Wild turkeys, blue jays, Steller's jays, scrub jays, wood ducks and red-bellied woodpeckers feast on acorn mast. The acorn woodpecker is named for its habit of collecting large quantities of acorns and storing them in "granaries," many small holes in trees, telephone poles and fenceposts. They are stored so tightly that a squirrel cannot get them out; the woodpecker will peck them out for use.

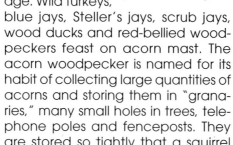

It's a Fact

❖ The Red Oak, also a member of the beech family, has open wood cells, providing a channel through the length of the wood. Try taking a piece of split Red Oak and sticking one end into a bucket of water. Hold your hands around the top end and blow through it. You will see bubbles rise in the water!

❖ Colonists used oak in the construction of barrels and water buckets. It also made strong beams for the construction of houses.

❖ Some species of oak, like the Interior Live Oak and Myrtle Oak, are evergreen, keeping their leaves all winter.

❖ The Gambel Oak, like most oaks, is common fuel wood where it is abundant.

Hall of Fame

The U.S. national champion Gambel Oak is 18 feet in circumference, 47 feet tall and has a spread of 85 feet. It grows in Gila National Forest, New Mexico. Several Beech family members are state trees. The White Oak honors Connecticut, Maryland and Illinois. The Live Oak represents Georgia.

Some Beech Family Members (see also Bur Oak)

Gambel Oak   Canyon Live Oak   Arizona White Oak   Blue Oak   Roble Oak   Chinquapin Oak   Little Post Oak

It's such fun to make leis from 'Ohi'a Lehua flowers for everyone at my birthday party.

'Ohi'a
'Ohi'a Lehua — Myrtle Family

Tree Traits

Habitat: 'Ohi'a Lehua (*Metrosideros polymorphia*) is native to the Hawaiian Islands, found between 1000 and 9000 feet elevation in a variety of conditions, including volcanic soil and tropical swamp, although it thrives best in moist, fertile soil. It is one of the first trees to establish itself and begin reforesting newly formed lava beds after volcanic eruptions. It is the most abundant native tree of the Hawaiian forests.

Height: Mature trees vary from merely a few inches to 100 feet.

Bark: It is fibrous and loose on mature trees, and brownish-gray.

Leaves: Thick, leathery and oval, leaves grow in pairs along the stem. They are up to $1^3/_4$ inches long, dull green above, pale below. New leaves are sometimes red. They are evergreen.

Flowers & Seeds: Small flowers grow in clusters, each with a long stamen making them look like festive, spiky pompons. They are usually red, but they can be pink, salmon, yellow, orange or white. Clusters can reach 3 inches in diameter. Flowers are followed by clusters of tiny seeds, in woody three-part pods, which are scattered by the wind.

Wild Companions

Many native island birds enjoy this tree. The crimson 'apapane darts quickly through 'Ohi'a Lehua branches, whistling as it goes. It feeds on the nectar and insects, thereby helping to pollinate the flowers. Its nest, built of twigs, ferns and forest moss, is often found in the 'Ohi'a crown. The curved-bill **'i'iwi,** a brilliant red bird, announces itself with loud, raspy squeaks, as it forages among the tree's blossoms for nectar. Lehua blossoms also attract bees.

It's a Fact

❖ Early natives used the durable wood of this tree for sacred temple carvings, spears, other weapons and tools. Bark was used to create black dye. Today the wood is used for railroad ties, flooring and furniture.

❖ Leis are a garland of flowers, traditionally given as a gesture of affection. Lehua blossoms have been a popular flower for leis on the main island of Hawaii for a long time.

❖ The size of this tree varies greatly, depending on habitat. Some trees, growing in boggy swampland, will reach no more than a few inches when mature. Others in rich, moist soil of the rain forest may reach 80 to 100 feet. Whatever the size, they are part of the tropical island beauty.

❖ Many young 'Ohi'a trees sprout on tree ferns. As they grow larger, they eventually strangle their host plant.

Hall of Fame

Lehua is the official flower of the islands of Hawaii. There is no official U.S. national champion 'Ohi'a Lehua tree.

Myrtle Family Members

'Ohi'a Lehua   Twinberry Eugenia   White-stopper Eugenia

Under the Palmetto I am a brave explorer sailing off to discover new worlds!

Palm
Cabbage Palmetto — Palm Family

Tree Traits

Habitat: The Cabbage Palmetto (*Sabal palmetto*) is found in native groves inland and on tidal flats and coastal sand dunes of the southeastern corner of the U.S., and extends into western Cuba and the Bahamas. It often grows in heavy thickets. It is also planted in other mild climates.

Height: The Cabbage Palmetto generally grows to 80 feet.

Bark: Sometimes smooth and sometimes rough, there are horizontal leaf scars that leave a cross-hatch pattern on the upper portion of the trunk. Right below the leaves, the trunk is sometimes partly covered by aged sheaths of fallen leafstalks.

Leaves: Also known as fronds, they are 4 to 8 feet long and fan-shaped with many narrow, pointed sections, divided almost to the center and drooping. There are stringy fibers along the edges. They are evergreen.

Flowers & Seeds: Small, sweet-smelling, white flowers, which hang in drooping 2 foot clusters that sprout from leaf bases, bloom in early summer. The round, black fruit, less than $1/2$ inch in diameter, ripens in autumn. Each sweet, shiny berry has one seed.

Wild Companions

Raccoons, robins and even black bears eat the fruit of the palmetto. Caterpillars of the palm skipper butterfly feed on Cabbage Palmetto. Black bears sometimes locate winter dens in heavy palmetto thickets. Red-bellied woodpeckers may hollow out nesting cavities in members of the palm family. The beautiful hooded oriole likes to hang its basket-like nest from the fronds of its West Coast relative, the California Washingtonia Palm. Leaves of a variety of palms provide safe cover for nesting birds.

It's a Fact

❖ Seminole and Choctaw peoples were among the Native Americans to use palmetto leaves to thatch the roofs of their houses. Tree trunks were also used in the construction of Seminole houses, which were called chickees.

❖ Palmetto leaf buds were harvested by the Seminole to eat like salad. These palm hearts, still taken from the crowns, result in the death of the tree. The small, sweet fruit was also eaten.

❖ Trunks were once used for construction of forts, docks and wharves. One such fort was the location of the famous Revolutionary War battle on Sullivan's Island, off the coast of South Carolina. On June 28, 1776, the British fleet was defeated when their cannon balls sank into the heavy palmetto-trunk walls of the fort. The victorious occasion is known as the Battle of Fort Moultrie.

Hall of Fame

The Cabbage Palmetto is the state tree of Florida and South Carolina. It is central to the design of South Carolina's state flag. The Cabbage Palmetto does not have an official champion.

Palm Family Members

Cabbage Palmetto

California Washingtonia Palm

Deer eat all the
persimmons they can reach.
Then I climb high up in my favorite
tree to pick the fruit for
spicy cookies.

Persimmon
Common Persimmon — Ebony Family

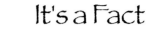

Tree Traits

Habitat: The Common Persimmon (*Diospyros virginiana*) is native to the southeastern portion of the U.S. It likes rich, moist soils, at elevations below 3,500 feet and is often seen growing along country roads and fences where seeds have been left by wildlife.

Height: The Common Persimmon generally grows to 80 feet.

Bark: Persimmon bark is blackish, scaly and alligator-like, divided into thick, square blocks.

Leaves: They are 3 to 7 inches long and leathery, dark green and shiny on top, lighter and fuzzy on the underside. They are deciduous.

Flowers & Seeds: Creamy to pale green, fragrant, bell-shaped flowers bloom in late spring. Male and female flowers grow on separate trees. Male flowers are smaller and in clusters. Female flowers grow individually. Round, orange to reddish-purple fruit is about the size of a plum when it matures in autumn. Fruit will still be hanging on bare trees in early winter after yellow or purplish leaves have fallen.

Wild Companions

Honeybees are drawn to persimmon blossoms in late spring. Black bears, raccoons, ring-tailed cats and opossums are among the mammals that harvest its sweet, orange fruit in the fall. They sometimes climb the tree to collect their meal. Eastern red foxes and skunks enjoy the fruit once it falls. **White-tailed deer** eat any fruit they can reach from the ground, and also enjoy nibbling the twigs and leaves. Wild turkeys and many other birds also enjoy this woodland treat.

It's a Fact

❖ Native Americans of the southeast ate the fresh fruit of the persimmon tree, dried it for winter food and used it to make bread.

❖ Persimmon wood is very hard, exceptionally strong and shock-resistant. Because of these qualities, it is used for golf-club heads, packing crates, textile shuttles and spools. It is a light creamy color with dramatic black or gray markings in the wood grain.

Hall of Fame

The U.S. national champion Common Persimmon title is shared by five trees. One found in Big Oak Tree State Park, Missouri, is 6³/₄ feet in circumference, 131 feet tall and has a 40 foot spread. The one from Dardanelle, Arkansas, is over 11 feet in circumference, 66 feet tall and has an 85 foot spread. The champ from Wayside, Mississippi, has an 8 foot circumference, is 110 feet tall and has a 54 foot spread. A Screven City, Georgia winner is 7 in circumference, and 121 feet tall with a 42 foot spread. There are two winners from Congaree Swamp National Monument, South Carolina. The first is almost 8 feet in circumference, 120 feet tall and has a 40 foot spread. The second is 7 feet in circumference, 132 feet tall with a 37 foot spread.

Ebony Family Members
Common Persimmon

Texas Persimmon

41

My sister and I like to play tag around our favorite giant Ponderosa. She can't catch me!

Pine

Ponderosa Pine — Pine Family

Tree Traits

Habitat: Ponderosa Pine *(Pinus ponderosa)* is widely spread throughout the western U.S. up to 8000 feet elevation, as well as in southwestern Canada and northern Mexico.

Height: Mature trees commonly vary from 60 to 180 feet.

Bark: In young trees the bark is black, maturing to rusty orange jigsaw puzzle-like "pieces" in old trees, with deeply etched, dark-colored furrows between the "pieces." The furrows can have a faint vanilla fragrance.

Leaves: Needles are usually 3 per bundle, 4 to 8 inches long, although there are several varieties of Ponderosa Pine which may have 2 to 5 needles per bundle. It is evergreen.

Flowers & Seeds: Male cones of the Ponderosa are tiny and soft, carrying pollen. Female cones are 2 to 6 inches long, egg-shaped with a sharp point or barb on the back of each cone scale. There are two winged seeds under each scale. Both cones grow on the same tree. Cones mature in the fall.

Wild Companions

Ponderosa Pine nuts provide meals for such birds as **Clark's nutcrackers**, scrub jays, evening grosbeaks and pine grosbeaks, and small mammals such as western gray squirrels, **Abert's squirrels** and western chipmunks. Red-breasted and white-breasted nuthatches scurry about upside down, foraging for insects on trunks and branches. Pines provide a nesting site for many birds, while others use pine needles or twigs as nest material. The stately bald eagle and the osprey construct large stick nests atop Ponderosas near water, where they fish.

It's a Fact

❖ Wintu, Shasta and Yurok peoples of northern California and southern Oregon used Ponderosa needles or roots in basketry. Cones were used as fire-starters. Pine nuts from various members of the pine family were used as food, although only the nut from the Pinyon Pine continues to be popular today.

❖ Tree cones in North America range in size from the Sugar Pine (up to 18 inches) to the Eastern Red Cedar ($1/4$ inch), and come in a variety of shapes.

❖ Lodgepole Pine was the most commonly used tree for tepee poles by native people of the Great Plains.

Hall of Fame

The Ponderosa Pine is the state tree of Montana. Many states honor other pines: Alabama and North Carolina—Longleaf Pine; Alaska—Sitka Spruce; Arkansas—Shortleaf Pine; Idaho—Western White Pine; Colorado and Utah—Blue Spruce. The U.S. national championship title for the Ponderosa Pine is shared by two trees. One in Plumas City, California is 24 feet in circumference, 227 feet tall and has a spread of 68 feet. The second is in Shasta-Trinity National Forest, California. It is 24 feet in circumference, 223 feet tall and has a 59 foot spread.

Some Pine Family Members (see also White Spruce)

Ponderosa Pine

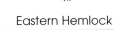

Eastern Hemlock

Singleleaf Pinyon

Eastern White Pine

In spring the Redbud flowers
make magical, soft pink clouds,
making me feel like an angel.

Redbud
Eastern Redbud — Legume Family

Tree Traits

Habitat: Eastern Redbud (*Cercis canadensis*) is found in much of the eastern U.S., southwestern Ontario and northern Mexico. The Redbud is an understory tree of mixed hardwood forests and cedar groves at low elevations.

Height: The Eastern Redbud generally grows to 40 feet.

Bark: Redbud bark is gray-brown, thin and smooth to flaky.

Leaves: Heart-shaped leaves are 2 to 5 inches in diameter and dark green. Leaves turn yellow before dropping in autumn.

Flowers & Seeds: Delicate pinkish-purple blossoms arrive in clusters in early spring. Leaves follow. Small, flat seed pods, about 2 to 4 inches long, will be reddish-black when they mature. Pods drop fall through winter. Sometimes a few stubborn ones cling to twigs even after the next season's flowers appear.

Wild Companions

The caterpillar of the tiny **woodland elfin butterfly** feeds on leaves of the

redbud tree. Bobwhite quail and some other birds eat the seeds. White-tailed deer browse tender redbud twigs and foliage. Several other members of this family provide browse for deer as well. Seeds that fall to the ground are sometimes eaten by rodents. Many members of this family, like Honey Mesquite, Paloverde and Catclaw, have flowers that attract honeybees.

It's a Fact

❖ Unpeeled reddish-brown twigs of California Redbud, a family member, were a colorful source of Native American basket material for such tribes as the Hupa, Miwok and Pomo of California. They were used with lighter materials to create contrasting geometric designs. Hunting bows were also made from the wood.

❖ Pods from the Honey Mesquite, another relative, were used by southwestern natives to grind into meal for cooking. Mesquite flour can be purchased today in health food or gourmet food shops.

❖ Blossoms of this tree are the source of a popular, mild honey.

❖ Because of its showy blossoms and colorful fall leaves, Redbud is popular as an ornamental tree in yards and public spaces throughout the U.S. George Washington, the first U.S. president, planted many redbud trees to adorn the landscape at his home, Mount Vernon.

Hall of Fame

This forest beauty is the state tree of Oklahoma. The Paloverde, another member of the legume family, is the state tree of Arizona. The Eastern Redbud has no official champion.

Some Legume Family Members (see also Honeylocust)

| Eastern Redbud | Velvet Mesquite | Catclaw Acacia | Western Redbud (California Redbud) |

My favorite tree is the
giant Redwood. It is so
big my whole family
together can't reach
around it.

Redwood
Coast Redwood — Redwood Family

Tree Traits

Habitat: The Coast Redwood *(Sequoia sempervirens)* has a native range limited to northern California and southern Oregon along the Pacific Coast at lower elevations where cool temperatures, coastal fogs and plentiful rainfall provide an ideal habitat. The tallest trees are located in fertile river-bottom land.

Height: The Coast Redwood grows to 300 feet, the tallest tree species in the world.

Bark: Coast Redwood bark is fibrous, furrowed and rust-colored, and as much as 12 inches thick.

Leaves: These flat and sometimes scale-like leaves are up to $3/4$ inch long, and pointed. They are deep green above, whitish below, and are evergreen.

Flowers & Seeds: Male and female cones appear on the same tree. Tiny male cones carry pollen. Oval female cones, barely over 1 inch at their largest, are a rusty color, and hang at the tips of twigs. Woody cone scales are thick and flattened. These tiny seeds will grow to become the tallest of all trees.

Wild Companions

The great blue heron may choose a redwood as a roosting spot, **osprey** and the endangered spotted owl nest high in standing dead trees. The black-tailed deer and Roosevelt elk rest and browse in their shade, and a variety of smaller wildlife finds shelter in healthy trees. Bats, chipmunks and flying squirrels are a part of this community. The raccoon may raise its young in the refuge of a fire-hollowed trunk, and the slimy banana slug slithers along fallen giants.

It's a Fact

❖ Though redwoods can grow from seeds, many of these forest giants rise up in halo-rings around the stumps of their ravaged ancestors. Wind-fallen redwoods give rise to rows of young trees. All of these new trees are clones of the original.

❖ The largest of redwoods are taller than the length of a football field.

❖ The Lolangkok Sinkyone were among the native people to live in the area of redwood forests. Their homes were conical or lean-to dwellings covered with redwood bark. Their canoes were made of hollowed redwood logs. Bark was woven into baskets as well as clothing.

❖ The reddish-colored wood is durable, knot free, and insect resistant, especially suitable for greenhouses, decks and garden furniture.

Hall of Fame

The Coast Redwood is the world's tallest tree. The U.S. champion Coast Redwood is 72 feet in circumference, 313 feet tall and has a spread of 101 feet. It is located in Prairie Creek Redwoods State Park, California. The Coast Redwood and the Sierra Redwood (also known as the Giant Sequoia) share the title of state tree of California.

Redwood Family Members

Coast Redwood

Giant Sequoia

Bald Cypress

The giant Saguaro is like a
desert apartment house for
our friends, the lizards, hawks,
and woodpeckers.

Saguaro
Giant Saguaro — Cactus Family

Tree Traits

Habitat: The Giant Saguaro (*Carnegiea gigantea*) is pronounced suh-WAR-o, and is the largest cactus in the U.S. It grows only in the desert regions of southwestern Arizona, southeastern California and northern Mexico.

Height: The Giant Saguaro commonly grows to 50 feet.

Bark: Saguaro bark is tough, yellow-green and waxy, with vertical accordion-like folds.

Leaves: This cactus has no leaves, but has clusters of sharp spines which may be as long as 2 inches.

Flowers & Seeds: Green buds begin to form crown-like clusters on the top of Saguaro trunks and arms in early spring. Waxy white blossoms appear in April and May, opening at night and closing by the middle of the following day. An open flower can be 3 inches across. Juicy, 3-inch tall egg-shaped fruits ripen in June and July. Each fruit may have as many as 2,000 tiny black seeds in its red flesh.

Wild Companions

Desert creatures flock to the Saguaro. The beautiful white-winged dove, honeybees and the endangered lesser long-nosed bat feed on the nectar of Saguaro flowers and pollinate them. Harris antelope squirrels, coyotes, javelinas, white-throated wood rats and a variety of birds eat the watermelon-colored fruit or its seeds. The regal horned lizard waits its turn for a tasty meal of ants that have come for the fruit that falls to the ground. Gila wood-peckers and **gilded flickers** hollow out holes in the trunks and branches, where they raise their young.

It's a Fact

❖ In a single rainstorm, the Saguaro can absorb and store 200 gallons of water—enough to survive for an entire year. As it takes in water through its shallow roots, its ribs expand, and accordion-like ridges on the surface of the Saguaro, stretch. The waxy surface protects against evaporation. A mature 150-year old Saguaro can weigh 16,000 pounds, much of which is water.

❖ The Tohono O'Odham people used the Saguaro for many purposes. The wooden ribs of dead Saguaro were used to build shelters and fences. The fruit was eaten raw, made into jam and used to make a ceremonial wine. Seeds were ground into a tasty butter. Saguaro ribs were made into stick dice; the dice were tossed and the player's score depended upon how they landed.

Hall of Fame

The elegant Saguaro blossom is the state flower of Arizona. The U.S. national championship is shared by several trees. The tallest is in Maricopa City, Arizona, with a height of 50 feet. The ones with the largest diameter (over 7 feet) and the widest spread (17 feet) are in San Manuel, Arizona.

Some Cactus Family Members

Barrel Cactus

Claret Cup Cactus

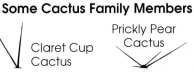
Prickly Pear Cactus

Saguaro Cactus

My favorite tree is
the sparkling Spruce tree.
On quiet snowy evenings
make a wish. It's my secre
wish-fulfilling tree.

Spruce
White Spruce — Pine Family

Tree Traits

Habitat: The White Spruce (*Picea glauca*) is native to evergreen forests through much of Alaska and Canada and into several of the most northern states of the U.S., to 5000 feet.

Height: The White Spruce grows to 100 feet.

Bark: Thin and silvery brown, the bark often has resin blisters.

Leaves: Aromatic, four-sided blue-green needles with sharp points are $1/2$ to 1 inch long and curve slightly upward on twigs. They are evergreen.

Flowers & Seeds: Pollen cones mature in late spring, releasing clouds of pollen. Female cones hang at ends of twigs and grow to a length of about two inches by fall, dropping from trees after they ripen. They are light brown with smoothly rounded cone scales. Each cone scale covers two winged seeds. Unlike fir needles, spruce needles are stiff and will roll between your fingers. Fir needles are flat, softer to the touch, and will not roll.

Wild Companions

Birds such as the pine siskin, red-breasted nuthatch, chickadee and the white-winged crossbill, as well as the red squirrel, eat seeds of the spruce family. The **spruce grouse** nests under the shelter of its low branches and eats its needles and buds. The snowshoe hare eats the bark during winter, and white-tailed deer browse twigs and foliage. Spruce groves provide

the dense shelter required for winter "deer yards" that protect white-tailed deer herds from blowing wind and snow and help them survive harsh weather.

It's a Fact

❖ The Tlingit, Makah and Haida peoples of the northwest were among those to use spruce roots mixed with maidenhair ferns in finely woven baskets with intricate and beautiful dyed designs.

❖ Small Black Spruce roots were split in half and used by Native Americans to stitch birchbark canoes and containers.

❖ Spruce wood is soft and lightweight, with straight grain. It is used for general construction and framing of buildings.

Hall of Fame

The U.S. national champion White Spruce is in Koochich City, Minnesota. It is 10 feet in circumference, 130 feet tall and has a spread of 28 feet. Many states honor members of the pine family: Maine and Michigan—Eastern White Pine; Minnesota—Red Pine; Nevada—both the Single-leaf Pinyon and the Bristlecone Pine; New Mexico—Pinyon Pine; Oregon—Douglas Fir; Pennsylvania—Eastern Hemlock; Washington—Western Hemlock; South Dakota—Black Hills Spruce.

Some Pine Family Members (see also Ponderosa Pine)

White Spruce

Tamarack

Black Spruce

Douglas Fir

I climb way up in the
Sweet Gum tree when we
play hide-and-seek.

Sweet Gum
Sweet Gum — Witch-Hazel Family

Tree Traits

Habitat: Sweet Gum (*Liquidambar styraciflua*) is found in low woodlands and rich riparian areas in the southeastern portion of the U.S., below 3000 feet. Sweet Gum is planted in many other areas as an attractive ornamental.

Height: The Sweet Gum grows to 120 feet.

Bark: This gray and scaly bark is deeply furrowed. Smaller branches may have cork-like, cracked wings or ridges extending lengthwise.

Leaves: Star-shaped leaves are usually five-pointed but sometimes seven-pointed, 3 to 6 inches long. They are dark green with long stems and finely toothed edges. Leaves make a colorful show of deep maroon, brilliant red, orange and yellow before dropping, until trees are decorated only with prickly seed pods.

Flowers & Seeds: Tiny, green male and female flower clusters grow on the same tree in spring. Fruit is a dangling one inch woody seed pod with many chambers and a stiff, spiny surface. Very small, winged seeds drop from open chambers when ripe in autumn. There are usually two seeds per compartment. Pods will hang on through much of the winter.

Wild Companions

The sweetleaf hairstreak butterfly lays her eggs on the twigs of Sweet Gum. After hatching, caterpillars feast on leaves and leaf buds. The tiny seeds attract a musical chorus of **American goldfinches**, pine siskins, purple finches, black-capped chickadees and a variety of other small birds. They peck enthusiastically at small openings in the dangling seed pods, reaching for the winged seeds inside. Seeds are also eaten by eastern gray squirrels and chipmunks. The hungry beaver dines on the bark of this and several other trees.

It's a Fact

❖ Cherokee used the sap of the Sweet Gum tree for chewing gum. Colonists chewed it and used it as medicine.

❖ In the early history of the American colonies, the Sweet Gum was taken across the ocean to European gardens. They used the balsam of this tree as an ingredient in perfume.

❖ Sweet Gum is widely planted as an ornamental in the United States because of its fast growth and dramatic fall foliage display.

❖ Sweet Gum wood is often stained to look like walnut or other more expensive woods. It is used for veneer, lumber and plywood.

❖ Seed pods of this tree are often used in combination with other dried plant material such as pine cones to make wreaths and other decorations.

❖ On breezy autumn days, dropping seeds make a pleasant sound like rainfall, as they tap against leaves on their way to the ground.

Hall of Fame

The U.S. national champion Sweet Gum is 23 feet in circumference, 136 feet tall and has a 66 foot spread. It is growing in Craven City, North Carolina.

Witch-Hazel Family Members

Sweet Gum

Witch Hazel

53

My favorite tree is the rope swing tree, a big old Sycamore that reaches way out over our swimming hole.

Sycamore
American Sycamore — Sycamore Family

Tree Traits

Habitat: The American Sycamore (*Platanus occidentalis*) grows in damp soil along streams, lakes and flood plains in the eastern U.S., at low elevations.

Height: The American Sycamore grows to 100 feet or more.

Bark: On bases of older trees the bark is rough, gray-brown and furrowed, becoming thin and smooth on the upper trunk and branches. Pale areas of white, cream, green, gray and brown fall off in large puzzle-like pieces.

Leaves: Bright green above and lighter below, leaves are 4 to 10 inches long. Their edges have large, scattered teeth with three or five pointed lobes. They are deciduous.

Flowers & Seeds: Very small, green flowers bloom in spring. Male and female flowers grow on the same tree. Round, green fruit balls, up to 1¼ inches in diameter, hang from very long stems. They mature to light brown in autumn. These dangling seed clusters stay on trees after fall leaves are gone. In winter they will come apart, releasing their small, hairy-tailed seeds.

Wild Companions

Purple finches feast on the small seeds of the American Sycamore, while water-loving birds like great blue herons can sometimes be seen roosting in upper branches of these riparian trees. The painted redstart forages for insects that hide under the Arizona Sycamore bark. Several species of hummingbirds build their tiny nests and raise their young in sycamore trees. Acorn woodpecker colonies drill holes in the soft wood of two relatives, the Arizona and California Sycamores to store their acorn supplies. They also nest in these large trees.

It's a Fact

❖ Hollow trunks of old sycamores sometimes provided emergency shelter for pioneers traveling in bad weather. They have the largest trunk of any North American hardwood, reaching almost 50 feet in circumference.

❖ Colonists made primitive buttons out of the hard centers of fruit clusters, still attached to a short piece of

branch by a durable stem. Thus, the common name for this tree is the Buttonball or Buttonwood tree.

❖ Sycamore wood is useful for butchers' blocks and food containers because it doesn't leave any taste or color on the food that touches it.

Hall of Fame

The U.S. national champion American Sycamore is almost 49 feet in circumference, 129 feet tall and has a 105 foot spread. It is located in Jeromesville, Ohio.

Sycamore Family Members

California Sycamore

American Sycamore

Arizona Sycamore

Somebody wanted to buy
Grandpa's Walnut trees to make into
furniture, but Grandpa wouldn't sell
them. He says lots of things are
more important than money.

Walnut
Black Walnut — Walnut Family

Tree Traits

Habitat: Black Walnut (*Juglans nigra*) is found in the eastern U.S. and in southern Canada along rich bottomlands, floodplains and streams in mixed hardwood forests. Needs well-drained soil.

Height: The Black Walnut grows to 100 feet.

Bark: Black Walnut bark is thick and deeply furrowed with scaly ridges, gray-brown to blackish in color.

Leaves: These leaves grow in stalks of 9 to 23 leaflets, each stalk measuring 8 to 24 inches. Leaflets are finely toothed and pointed, 2 to 5 inches each. They have a pungent odor and are deciduous. Leaves turn bright yellow before falling.

Flowers & Seeds: Spring brings small green flowers and young leaves to the Black Walnut. By summer nuts are beginning to develop. Round, creased, woody shells with fibrous green husks may be as large as 2 inches in diameter. There may be as many as three in a cluster. In autumn they will drop from the tree, ready for harvest. Nuts are sweet and oily.

Wild Companions

The richly flavored, nutritious, oily nuts of the black walnut tree, along with nuts of other family members like butternut, hickory and pecan, are eaten by eastern fox-squirrels, red and gray squirrels, **chipmunks**, black bears, deer, rabbits, ducks, wild turkeys, crows, bluejays and other hungry wildlife, including the red-bellied woodpecker. The caterpillars of hickory hairstreak butterflies and banded hairstreak butterflies rely on black walnut leaves for food.

It's a Fact

❖ Native Americans such as the Cherokee and Apache used the outer husk of nuts for brown dye. Black dye was made from the roots.

❖ Iroquois used hickory, a member of the walnut family, to fashion snowshoe frames because it is a very strong and shock-resistant wood. They also shaped it into bows, using a cord of deer sinew or hemp as the bow string.

❖ Colonial pioneers used Green Hickory for staves to secure wooden barrels and buckets. They used the inner bark to produce a yellow dye.

❖ The dark, richly grained, durable wood of the Black Walnut has long been prized for high quality furniture. Large old trees have become rare. Sometimes they are actually stolen.

Hall of Fame

The Pecan tree, a member of the walnut family, is the state tree of Texas. The U.S. national champion Black Walnut is on Sauvie Island, Oregon, and is 23 feet in circumference, 130 feet tall and has a 140 foot spread.

Some Walnut Family Members

Black Walnut

Arizona Walnut

Bitternut Hickory

Butternut

My favorite tree is
the Pacific Yew, the medicine
tree that helped Grandma
get well from cancer.
Thank you, Yew!

Yew
Pacific Yew — Yew Family

Tree Traits

Habitat: The Pacific Yew (*Taxus brevifolia*) is native to the Pacific Northwest portion of the U.S., western Canada and into the northern Rocky Mountains. It is an understory tree found in the shade of fir, spruce, Western Red Cedar and hemlock.

Height: The mature Yew varies from 10 to 60 feet.

Bark: Yew bark is thin, flaky and purple on the surface, with reddish new bark below.

Leaves: Flat needles are one inch or less in length, with stems slanting back in ridges along twigs. The upper side is dark yellow-green, while the under side is lighter. It is an evergreen.

Flowers & Seeds: Small green female flowers and smaller male pollen cones are found on separate trees. Each small flower becomes a pea-size, bright red cup. These soft, sweet cups are eaten by birds who then scatter the undigested purple or brown seeds. This ensures the spread of yew trees. Male pollen cones are light yellow.

Wild Companions

Birds like the white-winged crossbill eat the bright red fruit. Chickadees and other hungry birds hop about, foraging for the many insects that live on these trees. **Moose** and rabbits browse tender twigs, needles and bark in winter and early spring when food is scarce.

Thick foliage provides many birds with safe hiding places for nesting as well.

It's a Fact

❖ In the 1960s it was discovered that Pacific Yew bark contained the drug taxol, which has been found effective in treating some forms of cancer. Because it is a slow growing tree, bark harvesting put the Pacific Yew's survival in danger. Ways of producing taxol in the laboratory without destroying this important tree have since been developed.

❖ Native Americans of the northwest used this strong, durable wood for such things as harpoons and canoe paddles. It was also used to make sturdy hunting bows.

❖ Seeds and foliage of the Pacific Yew are poisonous to people.

❖ The heartwood is a beautiful rose color while the sapwood is pale yellow.

Hall of Fame

The U.S. national champion Pacific Yew is 15 feet in circumference and 54 feet tall, with a spread of 30 feet. It is located in Lewis City, Washington.

Yew Family Members

Pacific Yew

Florida Yew

California Nutmeg

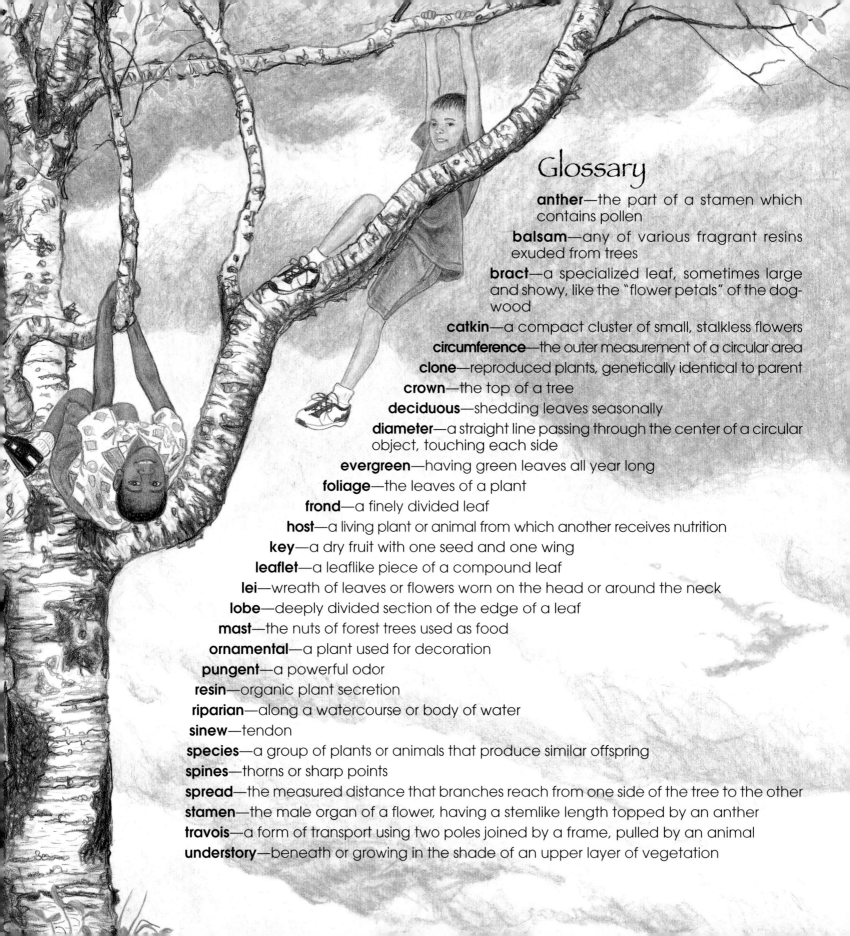

Glossary

anther—the part of a stamen which contains pollen

balsam—any of various fragrant resins exuded from trees

bract—a specialized leaf, sometimes large and showy, like the "flower petals" of the dogwood

catkin—a compact cluster of small, stalkless flowers

circumference—the outer measurement of a circular area

clone—reproduced plants, genetically identical to parent

crown—the top of a tree

deciduous—shedding leaves seasonally

diameter—a straight line passing through the center of a circular object, touching each side

evergreen—having green leaves all year long

foliage—the leaves of a plant

frond—a finely divided leaf

host—a living plant or animal from which another receives nutrition

key—a dry fruit with one seed and one wing

leaflet—a leaflike piece of a compound leaf

lei—wreath of leaves or flowers worn on the head or around the neck

lobe—deeply divided section of the edge of a leaf

mast—the nuts of forest trees used as food

ornamental—a plant used for decoration

pungent—a powerful odor

resin—organic plant secretion

riparian—along a watercourse or body of water

sinew—tendon

species—a group of plants or animals that produce similar offspring

spines—thorns or sharp points

spread—the measured distance that branches reach from one side of the tree to the other

stamen—the male organ of a flower, having a stemlike length topped by an anther

travois—a form of transport using two poles joined by a frame, pulled by an animal

understory—beneath or growing in the shade of an upper layer of vegetation

Organizations Concerned With Protecting Trees

This is a partial list of organizations that may be helpful to readers wanting to learn more about America's trees and how to protect them.

Ancient Forests International
P.O. Box 1850
Redway, CA 95560
717—923—3015

Write to get information about ancient forests and how to protect them.

Global ReLeaf
The American Forestry Association
P.O. Box 2000
Washington, D.C. 20013
202—955—4500

Write for information about tree planting projects.

Greenpeace USA
1436 U Street N.W.
Washington, D.C. 20009
202—462—1177

Write for information about how to protect the environment.

Kids for Saving Earth
P.O. Box 47247
Plymouth, MN 55447—0247
612—559—0602

Learn how to join with other kids to help save the Earth.

The National Arbor Day Foundation
100 Arbor Avenue
Nebraska City, NE 68410
402—474—5655

Get information about educational material and find out how to help plant trees.

National Forest Foundation
c/o J.L. Beasley
1099 14th Street N.W.
Ste. 5600—W
Washington, D.C. 20005
202—501—2473

Write for information about our National Forests.

Native Forest Network
c/o Philip Knight
P.O. Box 6151
Bozeman, MT 59771
406—585—9211

Ask for information about America's native forests and how to help protect them.

The Nature Conservancy
1815 N. Lynn Street
Arlington, VA 22209
703—841—5300

Write to find out how kids can help protect fragile habitats in their state.

North American Association for Environmental Education
1255 23rd Street N.W. #400
Washington, D.C. 20037—1199
202—884—8912

Write to ask about environmental education materials and programs that would be useful to your class or group.

Save the Redwoods League
114 Sansome Street, Room 605
San Francisco, CA 94104
415—362—2352

Ask what is being done to protect the Redwoods, and how you can help.

Sierra Club
P.O. Box 7959
San Francisco, CA 94120—9943
415—776—2211

Ask for information about local speakers who might be willing to visit your school. Request information about outdoor activities in your area.

Trees for Life
1103 Jefferson
Wichita, KS 61203
316—263—7294

Write for information about trees and how to help protect them.

Trees for Tomorrow
Natural Resource Education Center
519 Sheridan Street, East
P.O. Box 609
Eagle River, WI 54521
715—479—6456

Ask for information about educational materials on trees.

Tree Musketeers
136 Main Street
El Segundo, CA 90245
310—322—0263

Learn what kids can do to preserve trees.

Tree People
12601 Mulholland Drive
Beverly Hills, CA 90210
818—753—4600

Ask for information about tree planting projects.

Further Reading
about Trees of North America

A Tree in the Ancient Forest, Carol Reed—Jones, Nevada City, CA, Dawn Publications, 1995

All About Saguaros, Carle Hodge, Phoenix AZ, Arizona Highways, 1991

American Forests, "The National Register of Big Trees", a program of American Forests, P.O. Box 2000, Washington, D.C. 20013

American Wildlife and Plants: a Guide to Wildlife Food Habits, Alexander Campbell Martin, Arnold L. Nelson and Herbert S. Zim, New York, Dover Publications, 1951

America's Fascinating Indian Heritage, James A. Maxwell, editor, Pleasantville, NY, The Reader's Digest Assn., Inc., 1978

Encyclopedia of Native American Tribes, Carl Waldman, New York, NY, Facts on File Publications, 1988

Fall Color and Woodland Harvests, Ritchie C. Bell and Anne H. Lindsey, Chapel Hill, NC, Laurel Hill Press, 1990

First Americans, The, Josepha Sherman, New York, NY, Todtri Productions Ltd., 1996

Getting to Know Joshua Tree National Park, Patty Knapp, Moose WY, Children's Outdoor Library, M.I. Adventure Publications, 1996

Hawaii, A Floral Paradise, Leland Miyano, Honolulu, Hawaii, Mutual Publishing, 1995

Herbal Grove, The, Mary Forsell, Random House, Inc. 1995

Hummingbirds, Sara Godwin, New York, NY, Mallard Press, 1991

Indian Baskets, Sarah Peabody and William A. Turnbaugh, West Chester, PA, Shiffer Publishing Ltd., 1986

Indian Baskets of the Southwest, Clara Lee Tanner, Tucson, AZ, University of Arizona Press, 1983

Kachinas: a Hopi Artist's Documentary, Barton Wright, Flagstaff, AZ, Northland Press, 1973

National Audubon Society Field Guide to North American Trees, Elbert L. Little, Eastern Region and Western Region, Alfred A. Knopf, New York, 1980

National Geographic, "The Beauty and Bounty of Southern State Trees," William A. Dayton, Washington, D.C., Oct. 1957

National Geographic, "Wealth and Wonder of Northern State Trees," William A. Dayton, Washington, D.C., Nov. 1955

Trees of Hawaii, Angela Kay Kepler, Honolulu, Hawaii, University of Hawaii Press, 1990

Trees of North America, C. Frank Brockman, Western Publishing Company, Inc., 1968

Trees of North America, Phillips Roger, Random House, Inc., 1978

The Native Americans, Colin F. Taylor, editorial consultant, London, England, Salamander Books Ltd., 1991

About the Author/Illustrator

Diane Iverson hugs trees every chance she gets—"Doesn't everybody?" she says—especially Ponderosa Pines because they smell so good. She also swings on branches, tastes acorns and carries colored pencils and drawing paper on hikes. As a child, Diane's favorite tree was a black walnut behind her grandparents' barn near Kerman, California. Now as a visiting illustrator and author, she offers a cross-curriculum approach to nature studies, with an emphasis on Native Americans, pioneers, and the key role of trees in the web of life. This book is a natural branch of Diane's previous book, *Discover the Seasons*, also published by Dawn Publications.

OTHER DISTINCTIVE NATURE AWARENESS BOOKS FROM DAWN PUBLICATIONS

Discover the Seasons, by Diane Iverson. The unique spirit of each season of the year is vividly captured, and followed by hands-on seasonal activities and simple recipes.

I Celebrate Nature, by Diane Iverson, is an introduction to the wonders of nature for very young children.

The Tree in the Ancient Forest, by Carol Reed-Jones, in repetitive, cumulative verse, portrays the remarkable ways in which plants and animals living around a single old fir tree depend upon one another. Illustrated by Christopher Canyon.

With Love, to Earth's Endangered Peoples, by Virginia Kroll. All over the world, groups of people, like species of animals, are endangered. Often these people have a beautiful, meaningful relationship with the Earth, and with each other. This book portrays several of these groups of people, with love. (Teacher's Guide available.)

Lifetimes, by David Rice, introduces some of nature's longest, shortest, and most unusual lifetimes, and what they have to teach us. This book teaches, but it also goes right to the heart. (Teacher's Guide available.)

A Drop Around the World, by Barbara Shaw McKinney, follows a single drop of water—from snow to steam, from polluted to purified, from stratus cloud to subterranean crack. Drop inspires our respect for water's unique role on Earth. (Teacher's Guide available.)

This is the Sea that Feeds Us, by Robert F. Baldwin, links a seafood dinner enjoyed by a thankful family with the entire marine food web. Its cumulative verse is like waves that tie together the intricate chain of life in the sea.

A Walk in the Rainforest, by Kristin Joy Pratt, is a colorful, stimulating way of learning about the exotic animals and plants of the tropical rainforest. Written and illustrated when Kristin was 15 years old, this is the first of her popular trilogy, which also includes *A Swim Through the Sea* and *A Fly in the Sky.* (Teacher's Guides available.)

The **Sharing Nature With Children Series of Teacher's Guides** is distinctive in that they integrate character education with core science and language arts curricula.

Dawn Publications is dedicated to inspiring in children a deeper understanding and appreciation for all life on Earth. To order, or for a copy of our catalog, please call 800-545-7475. Please also visit our web site at www.DawnPub.com.